GW01044150

*Have you been
invited to all these
Sleepovers?*

Happy Birthday Sleepover Club

by Fiona Cummings

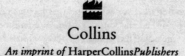

Collins

An imprint of HarperCollinsPublishers

First published in Great Britain by Collins in 1997
Collins is an imprint of HarperCollins *Publishers* Ltd
77-85 Fulham Palace Road, Hammersmith
London, W6 8JB

1 3 5 7 9 8 6 4 2

Text copyright © Fiona Cummings 1998

Original series characters, plotting
and settings © Rose Impey 1996

ISBN 0 00 675347 7

The author asserts the moral right to
be identified as the author of the work.

Printed and bound in Great Britain by
Caledonian International Book Manufacturing Ltd,
Glasgow G64

Conditions of Sale
This book is sold subject to the condition
that it shall not, by way of trade or otherwise,
be lent, re-sold, hired out or otherwise circulated
without the publisher's prior consent in any form,
binding or cover other than that in which it is
published and without a similar condition
including this condition being imposed
on the subsequent purchaser.

You are invited
to attend the

10th

Birthday Sleepover

Sleepover Kit List

1. Sleeping bag
2. Pillow
3. Pyjamas or a nightdress
4. Slippers
5. Toothbrush, toothpaste, soap etc
6. Towel
7. Teddy
8. A creepy story
9. Food for a midnight feast: something home-made, as practice for our Brownie Cook's badge
10. Torch
11. Hairbrush
12. Hair things like a bobble or hairband, if you need them
13. Clean knickers and socks
14. Change of clothes for the next day
15. Sleepover diary

PLUS: Surprise Birthday Gift

CHAPTER ONE

BOO! It's me. Kenny. You were expecting Frankie, right? Well, she couldn't come. She's ill. Not really, really ill, unfortunately. I could do with a proper patient to practise on. You can't train to be a doctor by operating on your sister's stuffed toys. But all Frankie Baby has is a bit of a temperature and a sore throat. Nothing to worry about. And not surprising either. You know how she can go on sometimes.

Phew! I'll just sit down for a minute and get my breath back. I was practising a few cartwheels before I got to you. Did you see me? The thing with cartwheels is that all the blood rushes to your head, then you go all kind of dizzy. It's quite nice actually. I was doing cartwheels here in this park when we thought of having the Sleepover Club birthday party.

It was at the beginning of the summer holidays. I was with the rest of the Sleepover Club and I was bored. I was bored because there was no football. I *live* for Leicester City Football Club, and I hate it in summer when the season has finished. But it wasn't just me, we were all feeling a bit bored. It's really weird because all we'd talked about for the last few weeks at school was what a great time we were going to have during the school holidays. We'd be sitting in the classroom struggling over some stupid maths problem, and one of us would say,

"Won't it be great when we can do

what we want, all day, every day!"

And then we'd all sort of daydream about how we were going to spend our summer holidays.

I'm the original 'Action Girl', I'm always on the move, so I imagined us playing rounders and doing lots of other outdoorsy things. I think Fliss fancied having lots of picnics in floaty dresses. P-lease! Lyndz and Rosie didn't seem to care what we did as long as the Sleepover Club did it together. Lyndz likes to get away from her brothers. (Fancy having *four* brothers! Still, I think I'd rather swap with her than have my stupid sister, Molly-the-Monster.) And Rosie just seems to enjoy hanging out with the rest of us.

It's hard to tell what Frankie wanted to do with her holidays. But whatever it was, she'd want to get the rest of us organised to do it too! She doesn't have any brothers and sisters, but you know that already don't you? We all know that because she never stops reminding us about it. She likes doing stuff with the Sleepover Club because she likes having other people to boss around! No, I'm only joking. Frankie's my best friend.

So, anyway, we had all these great plans for our summer holidays and three days into them we were bored. I mean seriously bored. Even a maths lesson followed by a spelling test would have been a treat. The thing is, everything seems to stop for summer. Everybody goes away and everywhere is really quiet.

"Do you think we're the only people in Cuddington who haven't gone away on holiday?" asked Frankie as we were lazing about in the park.

"Yet." said Fliss. "I'm going to…"

"Tenerife. In three weeks." The rest of us said together.

Fliss had told us about her holiday a zillion times already, and we weren't likely to forget.

"I was only saying!" grumbled Fliss and stomped off to the pond to look at the ducks.

"Get her!" laughed Lyndz.

"I wish I was going to Tenerife," moaned Rosie. "I wish I was going *anywhere*. We never go on holiday now."

Frankie, Lyndz and I pretended to play violins. We do that when Rosie is in one of her 'Poor-Little-Me' moods.

"We don't go on holiday much," said Lyndz. "There are too many of us. But I don't mind. There's always lots to do at home."

"But we used to go away a lot. Before dad left," mumbled Rosie. She looked as though she was going to cry. I'm not very good with people who cry. I don't know what to do with them. Lyndz is pretty good, and so is Frankie. I just don't cry very much myself. When I saw Rosie's lip going all wobbly, I thought it was a good time to see what Fliss was up to. She was probably still sulking, but we're used to that by now.

I wanted to see how many cartwheels I could do before I got to the pond where Fliss was standing. I thought it would be about twenty. One, two, three... twelve, thirteen, fourteen...

"Hey, watch it!" I cartwheeled right into Fliss and we both nearly ended up swimming with the ducks!

"Sorry Fliss," I spluttered. My head was in a major spin after being upside down so many times.

"You know Kenny," sighed Fliss, examining her legs for bruises. "You really are very clumsy."

She sounded like Mrs Weaver, our teacher. I wished I'd stayed with the others. Rosie crying would have been better than Fliss moaning.

"*And* I was trying to work something out before you nearly drowned me!" snapped Fliss.

She started muttering something and counting on her fingers. Fliss was certainly one strange dude!

Suddenly, she leapt into the air.

"I thought so. We've had nine! We've had nine!" she shouted.

Yep! That confirmed my original diagnosis – our Fliss had finally flipped!

"Nine what?" I asked. "Nine fights? Nine doughnuts? What?"

Frankie, Lyndz and Rosie had joined us. They had obviously seen the commotion Fliss was causing. What an embarrassment!

"What's she on about?" asked Lyndz. I shrugged my shoulders.

"We've had nine sleepovers!" Fliss shrieked. "That means that the next one will be our tenth!"

"Hey Fliss, go to the top of the class and give the teacher a banana!" I said. "I always knew that you'd learn to count one day!"

"Hang on a minute," said Frankie. "We've had loads of sleepovers. I'm sure we've had more than ten."

"I mean we've had ten since we formed the Sleepover Club with Rosie and everything," explained Fliss very slowly, as though she was talking to a bunch of three-year olds.

"Oh right," Frankie nodded.

"Anyway, as I was saying," continued Fliss. "Ten's an important number, isn't it? We ought to have a special sleepover to celebrate."

Yeah. One-nil! For once, Fliss was right. If we had a sleepover to plan, we couldn't get bored. Especially when it was a special birthday sleepover.

We all felt pretty excited and you know how hyper we can get. We all started talking at once, and laughing and doing high fives as though we'd all just won Olympic medals or something. Somehow I don't think we would have been so enthusiastic if we had known then what trouble this tenth sleepover was going to cause.

The thing is that we're all so different. And I know that that's a good thing, even though it has caused problems in the past. But we always managed to sort them out. And anyway, for our normal sleepovers we just sort of go with the flow, because it's the sleepover that matters and not really what we do there. But for this tenth birthday sleepover, boy did things get out of hand! It was like it wasn't just a sleepover anymore it was some major celebration. We all got very selfish and only wanted to do what *we* wanted to do. Crazy I know. I think we all went a little bit mad for a while.

"We should have a proper party, a dressed-up party, with music and dancing and a proper meal and maybe a marquee and..." said Fliss excitedly.

"What planet are you on Fliss?" I asked. "A marquee? The nearest you'll ever get to a marquee is the tent you sleep in at Brownie camp!"

"Alright Kenny Clever Clogs, what

do you think we should do for the sleepover?" Fliss snapped back. She had those bright-red patches on her cheeks, which is never a good sign.

"What about a day out at one of those paintball courses?"

The others all groaned.

"You only want to do that because you know you'd win. This has to be something special for *all* of us you know." I was surprised when Frankie said that. Us being best mates and everything.

"Alright then, what did you have in mind?" I asked.

"What about a children's party, with silly games and jelly and ice-cream, and balloons..."

"Don't you think we're a bit old for that?" asked Lyndz.

"That's the point," sighed Frankie, coming over all grown-up. "We don't have parties like that anymore because we *think* we're too old, but I think they're kind of fun."

"Oh please Frankie," moaned Fliss. "Everybody'd laugh at us if they ever found out!"

"What about going out to the cinema and having a pizza or something," asked Rosie.

"Bor-ing!" the rest of us sang together.

"I was only trying to help!" mumbled Rosie. "I know when I'm not wanted. I might as well go home."

She started walking towards the gate. The rest of us just watched her go. Then we all turned on each other.

"Now see what you've done!"

"What *I've* done. It was *your* fault."

"You always think you know best don't you?"

And before we knew where we were, we were all yelling at each other. And I mean *really* yelling. That's when it looked like the Sleepover Club would never even reach it's tenth birthday!

CHAPTER TWO

So, it was the summer holidays. We were bored. But now the Sleepover Club couldn't even be bored together because we weren't speaking to each other. Crazy hah?

I bet you've done that too haven't you? I mean, I bet you've fallen out with your friends over something really small and stupid. Only it seems really important at the time. It's only later that you realise how dumb the whole thing is. But by then it's too late. The damage is done.

It was awful. I felt totally miserable without the others. But somehow I just couldn't do anything about it. It hadn't been my fault that we'd fallen out in the first place, so why should I be the one to make up? Of course, if we'd all thought like that we would never have spoken to each other again. Frankie and I usually phone each other about a million times a day and we tell each other everything. When we fell out, we didn't speak for three days. Mum is always saying that I can never admit when I'm in the wrong, and I guess that's true.

Looking back it seems stupid that we let everything get so out of hand. But we have our diaries to remind us how awful we felt when we thought the Sleepover Club was about to split up.

I wrote:

If Fliss hadn't thought of having a tenth birthday sleepover party, we'd still all be speaking now. It looks like I'll be stuck with Molly-the-Monster all holidays. Pass the sick bucket! I wish we were going to stay with grandpa and grandma McKenzie now, rather than later in the holidays. At least I wouldn't be bored there. I'm bored bored BORED here without the others.

Frankie wrote in her diary:

Why is it we never agree on anything? If only we could have decided to have a normal party, then none of this would have happened. I don't see what was so wrong with my idea anyway. The others just don't like to do anything different. Well I'm not making the first move to get the Sleepover Club back together. I <u>always</u> end up having to organise everybody. And I'm sick of it.

Fliss wrote in hers:

Went shopping with mum today. She bought me a great pair of shorts and some yellow nail varnish. They're well cool! She said they were to cheer me up, but they haven't. I still miss the others.

Rosie scribbled in her diary:

I'm never going to make any friends again. Nobody likes me. Belonging to the Sleepover Club was great and now

I'm not sure whether there's even going to <u>be</u> one any more. (You couldn't read what else she'd written because the writing was all smudged where she'd cried over it. Breaks your heart doesn't it?)

Lyndz had just written:

Can't stand this anymore. I'm going to ring the others up and get them to meet round here tonight.

And that's just what she did.

It felt a bit weird at first going round to Lyndz's, knowing that there was this big 'thing' between us. We were just so polite with each other. It was as though some crummy old soap opera characters had taken over our bodies and we were sitting around discussing the price of tea or something. It was Frankie who sorted us all out – as usual.

"Look," she said in her grown-up tone of voice. "I'm sorry if I was stroppy the other day. I don't really mind what kind of party we have, as long as we all agree on it." The rest of us mumbled that that was how we felt too. We all looked at the floor, as though our feet were suddenly the most fascinating things in the world.

Suddenly, Lyndz leapt on to her bed and started bouncing on it.

"Come on guys!" she yelled at the top of her voice. "It's party time!" Yep! The Sleepover Club was back together. And just to prove it, Lyndz got hiccups.

"You do realise don't you, that we're the only people in the entire universe who know how to stop you making that appalling noise!" I said, as I dug Lyndz hard in the ribs. A shock like that sometimes does the trick.

"Ouch Kenny!" Lyndz doubled over. "Why do you think I got you all round here? Hic."

"Without us, you'd probably have to walk hiccuping down the aisle on your wedding day," laughed Frankie.

"I, Lyndsey, hic, Marianne, hic,

Collins, hic, do take you, Hic, Hic, Hic..." said Fliss, who knows the whole marriage service backwards.

"Except I'm never getting married," said Lyndsey. "My brothers are enough to put anyone off men for life!" The thought of getting married seemed to have stopped Lyndz's hiccups anyway. Either that or the fact that Frankie had been doing her 'thumb in the hand' routine on her for the last few minutes.

"OK then, so what are we going to do for this party?" asked Frankie when we'd all calmed down. "And where are we going to have it?"

Well, it was like feeding time in the monkey house: we all started chattering at once. And we got louder and louder. And because we were all shouting, nobody could hear what anyone else was saying.

"Shut up!" yelled Frankie. That girl could be a sergeant major with a voice like hers.

"Right," said Frankie, coming over all teacher-like. "If we decide where we're going to have the sleepover, we might be able to decide what we're going to do for it."

"My place would be good," said Fliss. "Because mum's ever so good at organising parties and stuff."

The rest of us weren't very sure about that. Fliss's mum would probably stand over us with a dustpan and brush in case we dropped any fairy cake crumbs on her precious carpet.

"I know my stupid brothers can get in the way," said Lyndz. "But we have got a big garden and my parents are pretty cool about letting us do our own thing."

That was true. But *I* wanted us to have the birthday sleepover at *my* place. That way I could organise a few wild, crazy games and the others couldn't do anything about it. The problem was Molly-the-Monster: the rest of the Sleepover Club dislikes her almost as much as I do – and that's lots!

"It'd be great if we had the sleepover at my place," whispered Rosie. "Adam loves you all coming round. And there are lots of rooms we could use."

Rosie has a stonking great house that her father was supposed to be doing up. He's not around much now, so it's chaotic and a bit run-down. But it's a pretty cool place to hang out. And the staircase is wicked for our 'sliding down the banister' races.

Still, we could have a sleepover there another time. I wanted the tenth birthday one at my place.

"OK, I'm like the rest of you. I'd like you all to come to my place," admitted Frankie. "My room's large, my parents are cool and we've always had pretty great sleepovers there in the past haven't we?"

"Are you saying that the sleepovers

everywhere else weren't much cop?" I asked. "What's wrong with my place?"

"Molly-the-Monster?" Frankie laughed. The others groaned. My stupid sister spoils all my fun.

"How can we decide on where to have it, if we all want it at our own place?" Fliss grumbled. "It's got to be fair!"

"Yeah, yeah, yeah," I moaned. Sometimes I get sick of Fliss going on about what's fair all the time.

"Just because you don't like doing the same things as the rest of us, doesn't mean that you can criticise us all the time," Fliss suddenly turned on me. "And have you ever thought that it might be *you* who's a bit weird for wanting to get all muddy and stinky rather than wearing make-up and having your hair nice?"

Well that was a shock! Fliss wasn't usually so aggressive.

"I'm just not into all that sissy stuff," I said.

"Sissy? That's not fair!" screeched Fliss.

"Fair! Is that all you ever talk about?" I shouted.

And suddenly we were at each other's throats again. This tenth birthday sleepover party looked doomed before the start! But I do admit that this time it was my fault.

"OK. Time out!" shouted Sergeant Major Francesca Thomas. "Have you two any idea what you look like? It's pathetic!"

Fliss and I stopped yelling and looked at each other. Her face was bright red and she looked *mad*! I must have looked like that too, because when we caught sight of each other we just cracked out laughing.

There was a knock at the door.

"I told mum that I'd need danger money to come into a room full of weird women!" Stuart, Lyndz's eldest brother, carried in a tray of orange juice and biscuits.

"Come on Lyndz. Shift some of this stuff from your desk. This tray is heavy you know." Lyndz is nearly as untidy as I am. There was so much stuff piled on her desk that when she tried to move it, it fell on to the floor.

"Hey what's this?" asked Rosie, picking something up.

"Oh that's just a card I'm working on for my Artist's Badge at Brownies," said Lyndz taking it from her.

"Oh no! I'd forgotten!" gasped Rosie. "I'll have to start planning it tonight. What else do we have to make? Is it a bookmark?"

"Or a poster," said Fliss.

I hadn't even thought about what I was going to make, and the Badge Tester was coming to Brownies the following Thursday.

"That's it!" shrieked Frankie, grabbing me by the shoulders. "I've done it again! I am a genius!"

"Oi! Let go of me Big Head!" I gasped. "What cunning plan have you thought of now?"

"Well," spluttered Frankie. "We're all doing the Artist's Badge right? If we all design a birthday card for the Sleepover Club, then get the Tester to decide which one is the best, whoever designed the best card gets to hold the tenth birthday sleepover party. I told you I was clever didn't I?"

Frankie was talking so fast that all her words had fallen over each other. So it took the rest of us a little while to work out what she had said. But when we did, we had to admit that the girl's got brains.

Of course, we still had the problem of deciding exactly what we were going to do at this party. But first we were all determined to win the competition.

CHAPTER THREE

After Frankie had had her brainwave we were all eager to get home to design our creative masterpieces. The trouble is that I'm about as good at drawing as an elephant is at roller-skating. If we'd been competing for something like the Athlete's Badge, then I would have started putting up the party streamers. As it was, I knew that I would be going somewhere else for the tenth birthday sleepover party. The question was, where?

My money was on Lyndz winning the competition. She's brilliant at making things. I can sort of see things in my head, but when I try to put my ideas down on paper, they come out all wrong. Lyndz seems to have good ideas, *and* be able to carry them out. Fliss is very prissy and fussy about things. They never quite turn out as she expected them to, but they are always very neat and tidy. And adults always like that don't they?

Frankie is a bit hit-and-miss. Once in art at school, she made this really great dinosaur out of papier-mâché. It was wicked. It stood outside Mrs Poole's office for weeks. Parents would come into school and stand for ages admiring it, like it was by some famous sculptor or something. Then the next time Frankie made a model it was worse than one of those piles of junk you bring home when you're in nursery class. She can be weird like that. You never know what to expect.

I'd never really seen much that Rosie had made. Her last sleepover invitation was pretty neat. But Adam had helped her design it on the computer, so that didn't really count. All I knew for sure was that although I had tried my best with my birthday card, it wasn't going to be good enough to win our competition.

We all met up at Frankie's house a couple of days before Brownies. All the others seemed very confident that their card was going to be the best. But everybody acted like their design was the biggest secret in the universe. Frankie had even asked her father to lock hers away in his filing cabinet. I ask you, how ridiculous can you get?

"If it's a birthday sleepover, are we going to buy presents?" asked Lyndz.

"Oh, we've got to, I love presents!" said Fliss. "This is great. It means we'll all have two birthdays. Like the Queen."

"Hang on one second!" I said, putting on a cheesy American accent. "I mean I love you guys and everything, but I have a serious shortage of dosh. You know what I'm saying?"

"Me too," admitted Rosie. "I never seem to have any money."

Frankie and Lyndz agreed.

A brainwave suddenly hit me:

"Why don't we just give one present each? We don't need to buy it either, we could make it," I said. "I'm sure I could knock something up out of a washing-up bottle and a bit of string. I've seen 'Blue Peter' often enough!"

Who says Frankie should have all the bright ideas?

"I know it's the thought that counts," laughed Lyndz. "But would we really want something you'd made, Kenny?"

The cheek of it! I couldn't let her get away with that. I wrestled her to the ground until she was hiccuping and begging for mercy.

"I'd, hic, love anything you made, hic, Kenny! Really I would!" she spluttered.

"But how would we decide who we were getting the present for?" asked Rosie whilst Frankie dealt with Lyndz's hiccups. She tried a cold marble down her T-shirt for a change. And it worked!

"We could have a lucky dip," said Frankie. "We'll all write our names on a piece of paper, put them in a hat and pull one out. As long as no one picks their own name, it'll be cool."

"And we could keep it a secret. Whose name we've got I mean," said Lyndz. "Then when we get the presents at the party, we'll all have to guess who bought them."

"That means we'll all have to wrap them in the same paper and put them in a special place at the sleepover when nobody else's looking," said Frankie. She always thinks of things like that.

We were all pretty excited about our presents. We each wrote our names on scraps of paper, which Frankie tore out of a notebook. Then she got out her favourite purple velvet hat, and we put all the pieces of paper in it. We each took it in turns to pull out a name. I was the last to pick, so there was only one left. It said:

Fliss

I looked round to try to figure out who had picked my name, but everyone was shoving the papers in their pockets, and had sort of secret smiles on their faces.

"I've seen some great earrings in that shop in the village," said Fliss. "I just thought it might help to give someone a few ideas!"

Oh great! Now we'd have to listen to Fliss dropping hints about her present right up until the sleepover. And we didn't even know when that would be.

"Call me picky..." I said

"Hello Picky!" said the others together.

"Ha! Ha!" I said. "What I was going to

say was, call me picky but it would be nice to know when we're going to have this sleepover. Some of us have lives to plan you know!

"Right! You mean your hectic social life of showbiz premieres and parties I take it!" laughed Frankie.

"I wish!" I said. "I just want to know, that's all."

"Well, I say we should wait until after Brownies on Thursday," said Frankie. "At least then we'll know whose house the sleepover's going to be at. Everything else should be easy to decide after that."

"Right as usual Batman!" I said.

We never usually take this long to plan our sleepovers. I was beginning to think that this one would never happen.

When we saw each other at Brownies on Thursday, we finally showed each other the cards we had been working on for the Artist's Badge. Mine was by far the worst, but that was no surprise. The others were good, but as soon as we saw all our cards together, it was obvious who would be holding the sleepover.

For the Artist's Badge we could design any kind of card. Frankie, Fliss, Lyndz and I had just made ordinary birthday cards. Rosie had made a special *'Happy Tenth Birthday Sleepover Club'* card, complete with a badge.

Coo-ell!

"Wow, Rosie. That's brilliant!" I said.

"You're bound to win! Yours is the best card by miles," said Frankie.

"Thanks very much!" said Fliss.

Frankie ignored her.

"Why don't we just agree that the tenth birthday sleepover will be at Rosie's place?"

Lyndz and I nodded. But Fliss wasn't having that.

"You said that we would ask the Tester to judge the cards," she moaned. "So that's what we should do. She might like something different."

"Like yours you mean?" I asked.

"Maybe," said Fliss.

When we saw who was testing us for our Artist's Badge, we realised why Fliss had been so keen to wait for her opinion. It was Sally Davies, Snowy Owl's best friend. And as I'm sure you remember, Snowy Owl is none other than Fliss's auntie, Jill!

We'd had to do other things for the badge, besides our card. We'd had to design a pattern in three colours and paint or draw a picture. As well as the card, I'd made a bookmark. (I'd painted fluorescent squiggles on it with some of Molly's special paint. She wasn't very happy about that. One-nil!)

Sally looked at all our things separately, then all the Brownies who were taking the badge had to sit at a table together and draw a vase of flowers. I went for the big and colourful look, the others copied what they saw. But that's art isn't it? Everybody looks at things differently.

Sally seemed pleased with everybody's work. She complimented me on my 'bold' style, which sent Frankie into hysterics. When Sally had signed all our forms to say that we had gained the Artist's Badge, Frankie explained about our cards and about the competition we were holding.

"Would you just tell us which card is the best?" she asked.

We'd laid them all out on the table, so it wasn't obvious who had made each one. Although of course she had seen them before and could probably remember.

"I'm not sure that picking out one from the rest is a good idea girls," said Snowy Owl. "You know that everybody's work is as valuable as everybody else's."

We all rolled our eyes to the ceiling.

"No really Auntie Jill, we want Sally to choose," explained Fliss. "We can't decide where to hold our next sleepover, and whoever made the best card gets to hold it at her house. So you see, we really need her help."

Frankie and I nearly cracked up when she said 'Auntie Jill' in that sweet way of hers. She was obviously trying to influence Sally's decision.

"Alright then," said Sally, picking up all the cards and looking at them very carefully. "I think you've all done a fantastic job. But I have to say that this one really stands out because it's so different."

She picked up Rosie's card.

"Putting the badge on there was a very clever idea."

We all patted Rosie on the back. All except Fliss, who scowled at Snowy Owl.

So we finally knew that our tenth birthday sleepover was going to be held at Rosie's house, and that was pretty cool. Not only does she have a humungous house with about a million rooms, but her mum is really great, really young and trendy and a real laugh. The best bit though, is that we can actually write on Rosie's bedroom walls!

I really thought that once we knew where the birthday sleepover was going to be held all our problems were over. How wrong can you be! They were only just beginning!

CHAPTER FOUR

You know the story of Dr Jekyll and Mr Hyde, where the guy has two completely different personalities? Well that was Rosie as soon as she knew that the birthday sleepover was going to be at her place. She was like some power-crazed monster. No one had ever seen her like that before. And I'm certainly not in a hurry to see her like that again.

We all met up at the shops in Cuddington on the Saturday after Brownies. They're easy for us all to get to, apart from Lyndz who lives a little bit further out than the rest of us. And our parents are quite happy for us to go there by ourselves. You know what parents are like! Always worrying about something. But at least they know we're safe there. Apart from the threat of Fliss driving us all crazy by telling us about some great earrings she's just seen, and the cool nail varnish she 'just has to have'. P-lease!

We always meet on the same bench outside the newsagents. Rosie was the last to arrive. When she did appear, she was carrying a mountain of paper.

"What on earth have you got there?" asked Lyndz.

"Plans for the sleepover. Is next Saturday alright?" asked Rosie, flopping down next to us.

"Now, let me just consult my diary," I said, pretending to flick through some imaginary pages. "Let me see. Next Saturday you say? Hmm. I think I can squeeze you in!"

"Sounds good to me!" said Lyndz.

"Fine by me," agreed Frankie.

"So we've got a week to sort the presents out!" said Fliss. The rest of us groaned.

From the pile she was carrying, Rosie pulled out four invitations. Pinned to each one was a copy of the badge she'd made for Brownies.

Rosie invites you to the special

10th

BIRTHDAY SLEEPOVER
at
75 Welby Drive
Welby Avenue
Cuddington Leicester

Please come at 5pm on
Saturday 27th July
Be prepared to
PARTY!

"Cool!" we all gasped.

"Adam did these on the computer for me. I thought it would be nice if we could all wear one for the sleepover," she seemed very pleased with herself. "All you've got to do is cut them out and make them into a badge. Is that OK?"

"Yep, I think even we can manage that!" I laughed, pulling a face at Frankie.

"Now," said Rosie, reading from one of her larger sheets of paper. "What I thought was: arrive at 5pm, put things in my room until 5.15pm, games outside until 6.15pm, make-up and hair, (possibly a fashion show if we can fit it in) until 7pm, food until 7.45pm, Twister until 8.15pm, then disco until mum sends us to bed, which she says will be about 10pm – if we're lucky! Washing and undressing until 10.30pm, giving out presents until 11pm, then midnight feast. Everybody OK with that?"

We were all sitting round with our jaws scraping the pavement. Was this girl for real? This was more like a military exercise than a sleepover. It was supposed to be *fun* for goodness sake!

"Erm, Rosie, I think you've forgotten one thing," I said very seriously.

"No, I can't have. I was up all night planning this. What have I forgotten?" she said, furiously reading through her timetable.

"What about toilet breaks?" I giggled. "I mean what if we need to go to the loo in the middle of the outdoor games? Should you plan for us to all to go together just to be on the safe side? Then we won't mess up your timetable."

"Like at school you mean?" Rosie looked very thoughtful. "That's not a bad idea. I'll see where I can fit it in." The rest of us cracked up. Even Fliss knew that I was joking and Fliss has a sense of humour the size of a pea.

"And I'm not sure about the beginning bit," said Lyndz. Rosie flicked through her notes. "You mean 'arrive at 5pm put things in my room at 5.15pm?' What's wrong with that?"

"Well what if one of us is late? Or it takes us longer to get our stuff sorted out?" asked Lyndz.

"Yes and where are we going to put the presents so the others can't see them?" asked Fliss.

"Oh no!" gasped Rosie. "I've got to do some more planning. But you can't be late. You just can't be. It'll mess everything up if you are!" She looked as though she was going to cry.

"Don't you think you're taking this a bit seriously?" asked Frankie gently.

"I just want it all to be perfect, what's wrong with that?" snapped Rosie. "It's not just any old sleepover. It's our tenth birthday sleepover and I want to make sure we'll all remember it."

She was certainly right about that. I don't think any of us will ever forget it!

"Is there anything you want us to bring?" I asked. "Stopwatches, so we don't run over time? Running shoes so we can sprint from one thing to another?"

"Party clothes? Balloons? Cuddly toy?" asked Frankie.

"What about the cake?" asked Fliss. "We've got to have a cake."

Rosie began to search frantically through all her sheets of paper.

"The cake!" she shrieked. "How could I forget about the cake?"

It was a bit sad really, seeing her get so upset.

"Don't worry. We could buy one," I suggested.

"We've no money," Lyndz reminded me.

"Well let's make one then!" Frankie said.

Now the Sleepover Club are not exactly the greatest bakers in the world. In fact, we are a total disaster in the kitchen.

"Is that a good idea?" asked Fliss. Her mum never lets her loose in their gleaming white kitchen. Not after we nearly burnt the place down anyway.

"Sure it is!" said Lyndz very confidently. "My mum's a mean cook. She'll give us a hand. She likes getting the chance to do stuff like that. She's always complaining that my brothers aren't interested in anything domestic. And neither am I, usually."

"We'll have to do it before next Saturday," Rosie reminded her. "Is that OK?"

"No probs," said Lyndz. "I'll ask mum when I get back this afternoon and give you a ring. You can all come over to my place and we'll have a girlie afternoon in the kitchen!"

Now I don't know about you, but cooking isn't really my thing. Eating, yes. Cooking, no way. But what could I do? I couldn't let my friends down now, could I? So when Lyndz rang that evening to say that we could all go there on the Friday before the sleepover to bake the cake, well how could I refuse?

Anyway, before that I had other things on my mind – like what to give Fliss for her stupid sleepover birthday present!

I know that this sounds really mean, but I really resented having to spend my pocket money on something which Fliss would like for five minutes and then throw away. She's like that is Fliss. She has to have all the latest fashions she sees in magazines, then when the next thing comes along, she forgets how desperate she was for this skirt, or that pair of trainers, and she wants something else. Frankie reckons that I'm jealous, but it's not that. I'll be quite happy wearing my Leicester City football shirt until I die. I don't like frills and sequins like Fliss. And I don't really care how I look.

I know it sounds really petty, but I didn't want to buy her the earrings that she liked, just because she'd hinted that she wanted them. That would have felt like she'd won. I was determined to give her something different. And I wanted to make it myself, just to prove that I could.

I rummaged about under my bed. I was bound to find something useful there. I found piles of old football magazines, a couple of stinky socks which didn't match, a baby's dummy (I have no idea where that came from) and a length of clear plastic tubing. I couldn't remember where I'd found the tubing, it was just something that I thought might come in useful one day!

I didn't think Fliss would be very impressed by hand puppets made out of the socks. And I wasn't going to sacrifice my football magazines for anybody. I picked up the tubing. It was so long that I could use it as a skipping rope. It was ages since I'd skipped. It was pretty cool!

"Watch it! You'll go through the floor!" snarled Molly-the-Monster as she came into the room. "What is that anyway?"

"Plastic tubing," I said showing it to her.

She wrapped it around her waist, then draped it around her neck.

"What do you want it for?" she asked, looking at herself in the mirror.

"Dunno. Something," I shrugged.

"If you decide you don't want it, I'll have it," she said, and slammed the door behind her as she went out.

That settled it. If Molly thought that the tubing was worth having, then I was going to keep it for Fliss's present.

I still wasn't sure what I was going to do with it though. I had some glitter left from the card I'd made for my Artist's Badge. I held the tubing so there was only a short length, and poured some glitter into it. It looked brilliant, even if I say so myself. It was exactly the kind of thing that Fliss loves. So that's when I decided to make her some glittery bracelets for her present.

When I had finished, I was well pleased with my efforts. Even Fliss should be kind of impressed. And no way would she ever suspect me of making the bracelets.

So then there was a long boring week until the Friday when we all met up again at Lyndz's for the great birthday cake bake. And what an event *that* turned out to be.

CHAPTER FIVE

If I'm honest, I wasn't looking forward to the cooking party at Lyndz's. I enjoy being with the others and everything. And Lyndz's mum is great. It's just *cooking*! You know what I'm saying?

Frankie had organised which cake ingredients we should each take to Lyndz's. I had the huge responsibility of providing the flour.

"You do know that it's self-raising flour we need, don't you Kenny?" Frankie asked over the phone.

"You mean it can lift itself off the

shelf, all by itself?" I asked really innocently.

"You are joking, right?" she asked.

"Of course I am, dummy!" I laughed. "I may not be into baking, but I think I know what kind of flour we need for a cake!"

So, on Friday afternoon, I arrived at Lyndz's armed with a bag of flour. I thought that at least if things got really bad, I could make flour bombs with it. Although I don't think Lyndz's mum would have been too thrilled about that.

I was the last to arrive. The others were already in the kitchen with their hair tied back and their pinnies on. Aw, sweet!

"Here she is! Our vital ingredient!" laughed Lyndz's mum when she saw me.

"That's me!" I said. "You can't do anything without Laura McKenzie!"

I put the bag of flour down on the work surface next to the butter, the sugar, the icing sugar and the eggs.

"Have you got an apron?" Lyndz's mum asked me. The others spluttered with laughter.

"Kenny? Wearing an apron? You must be joking!"

"I hope you don't spoil your football shirt," said Lyndz's mum seriously.

"How can she spoil it when it already looks like an old dishcloth?" asked Frankie. I strutted around the kitchen as though I was modelling an expensive ball-gown in a fashion show.

Then the others went into Delia Smith mode. (I'm not going to bore you with all the details. Baking a cake isn't the most exciting thing in the world. I'll just give you 'Kenny's edited highlights' of the afternoon, which is all you really need to know.)

After the others had weighed out the butter and sugar and put them into a bowl, Lyndz asked her mum if we could use the electric whisk.

"Yes, but be careful. Are your hands

dry?" She felt all our hands. "OK. Turn it on at the mains, then turn the whisk on gently to start with and keep the beaters in the bowl. Whilst one of you does that, someone else can be breaking those two eggs into a bowl. Careful not to let any shells in. When you've done that give them a good whizz together with a fork. Now that's you lot sorted, you haven't seen Spike anywhere have you?"

Spike is Lyndz's baby brother. I think even I would have noticed if a baby had been crawling around the kitchen floor.

"Let me have a go! Please can I use the whisk?" begged Fliss.

"What are you like Fliss?" asked Frankie. "Is using an electric whisk the biggest thrill of your life?"

Fliss does tend to get a bit excited about weird stuff like whisks!

"This is cool!" she laughed.

Lyndz's mum disappeared again on the track of Spike. It's usually quite easy to find him: you just follow the trail of biscuit crumbs.

I was getting a bit bored. Fliss looked very serious. The temptation was too much. I sneaked up behind her and, yelling "Gotcha!", I tickled her under the arms. Fliss jumped a mile and forgot that she was holding the whisk. She lifted it out of the bowl and mixture flew everywhere.

"Turn it off!" yelled Frankie, who almost dropped the bowl of eggs she was beating.

"I can't!" shouted Fliss who seemed to have completely lost control.

The whisk suddenly stopped whizzing. Lyndz had turned it off at the mains.

"You stupid idiot!" yelled Fliss, turning on me.

"I'm sorry," I said. "I didn't know that was going to happen."

We looked round the kitchen. Everything was covered in tiny splatters of creamed sugar and butter.

"We ought to try and clean some of this up before your mum comes back," said Frankie. She grabbed a dishcloth and started to wipe up the worst of the mess. The rest of us grabbed kitchen roll and started to do the same. I couldn't help grinning to myself: an electric whisk was a pretty cool weapon.

By the time Lyndz's mum re-appeared, the worst of the mess was gone and the others were dropping tiny bits of egg into the mixture and giving it a good stir. Yawn, yawn, how boring!

Next we sieved the flour. I hadn't helped with the baking at all so Frankie made *me* hold the sieve. She said that even I couldn't get that wrong. And it really wasn't my fault when I covered everyone in flour. It was Spike's! He charged right into me and the sieve flew out of my hand. It was like a snowstorm! Fortunately Lyndz's mum knew it wasn't my fault.

But that didn't stop the others from having a go at me – especially Fliss. Her hair was covered in flour. She looked like someone's granny!

"If you're not doing anything Kenny," said Frankie, "you might as well make a start on the washing-up!" Charming!

"Right sir!" I shouted like a soldier and saluted to her. Frankie grinned.

I was up to my elbows in dirty dishes and bubbles when Lyndz's brother Ben appeared. I didn't see him dropping pieces of Lego into the cake mixture. I didn't see him trying to feed it to Buster, the dog. But I did feel it on the back of my neck when he threw a handful at me.

"Oi! What are you doing you horror?" I shouted.

The others were already yelling and fishing the Lego out of the cake. They were not happy bunnies.

"Go to Mum!" Lyndz shouted. Even *she* can lose her cool sometimes.

The last thing we had to do was pour the mixture into the two tins. That was not as easy as it sounds, but we managed it in the end. And Buster ate all the dollops that fell onto the floor, so they didn't really matter.

"Mum! We're ready to put them into the oven now!" yelled Lyndz. She's another who could be a sergeant major!

Stuart appeared.

"Mum says I've to put them into the oven for you," he said. He stuck his finger into one of the tins. "Hmm. Not bad!"

"Aw Stuart!" moaned Lyndz. "We took ages smoothing the top of that. Now we'll have to do it again."

"Well hurry up," grumbled her brother. "I've got to leave for the farm in a minute."

"Be careful they don't mistake you for one of the pigs, won't you!" laughed Lyndz.

"Ha, ha!" said Stuart. "Do you want

these in the oven or not?" He took the tins from Lyndz and put them on the middle shelf in the oven.

"Save me a bit of cake won't you?" he called as he left. "I did play a vital role in making it!"

We ignored him.

"The recipe book says '25–30 minutes cooking time'," read out Lyndz. "Who can remember that? What time is it now?" Lyndz is hopeless at telling the time, so we all looked at our own watches.

"Ten past four," we all said together.

"So we should look at the cake at twenty-five to five then," said Frankie.

Lyndz looked very confused, but the rest of us agreed.

When we'd finished the rest of the washing-up and had cleared away, we messed about with Spike and Ben. Then we went out into the garden.

"How's your cake doing?" Mrs Collins called out to us. We all looked at each other. The cake! We'd forgotten all about it! It was almost ten to five. We raced inside. The kitchen was filled with sort of a thick, not quite a burnt smell.

"Quick! Mum! We'll have to get the cakes out now!" yelled Lyndz.

"Don't panic!" laughed her mum, opening the oven door. "There now. They look great!"

They didn't look great exactly. But they didn't look too bad. And when they'd cooled and we'd sandwiched them together with jam and put icing on top, the birthday cake looked all right.

We all shared the icing bit. It read:

Happy Birthday
Sleepover Club

Now we were all set for the party.

CHAPTER SIX

I woke up really early on Saturday morning. It wasn't just excitement that woke me, it was something else as well – rain. It was pouring down. Not only that, but it was windy too. I couldn't believe it! Until then every day had been warm and sunny. Now it felt more like November than the middle of July! Miserable or what?

"Your stupid sleepover party's going to be a bit of a washout. What a pity!" laughed Molly-the-Monster peeping out from her duvet.

"Shut up!" I yelled and hit her with

my pillow. She's only jealous because I go to more sleepovers than she does.

"Ouch! That hurt!" she screamed and thwacked me with her own pillow. "At least I'll be able to get some peace and quiet in my *own* room tonight."

I wish that we lived in a house like Rosie's, then I could have my own bedroom. I hate sharing a room with Monster Features.

The rain didn't stop all day. I kept looking out of the window to check. By 4.30pm it was raining so heavily that I expected to see Noah floating past the house in his ark!

"Looks like you're going to have a wet one, love!" said Mum as I climbed into her car. "You have packed enough warm things, haven't you?"

"Yes Mum!" I sighed, as I pinned on my 'Happy Tenth Birthday Sleepover Club' badge. She'd asked me that about a thousand times already.

We usually walk to sleepovers, especially in the summer. We don't live very far from each other, as you know. But seeing as it was so wet, mum had arranged to give Frankie a lift to Rosie's. Lyndz and Fliss were going together.

"Poor Rosie," said Frankie as she got into the car. "I bet she hadn't planned for rain."

"Oh, I don't know," I said. " Now the timetable probably says 'Come in and drip in the hallway until 5.01pm, remove raincoats until 5.02pm, then water sports in the garden until 5.37 precisely'."

Frankie and I both giggled.

"I hope you're not being unkind, Laura McKenzie," said Mum. "I think Rosie sounds like a very organised young lady, and it wouldn't do you any harm to take a leaf out of her book!"

"Aw, Mum!" I groaned. "It's so boring!"

We pulled up outside Rosie's house. Two pathetic balloons were dangling from the gate. They made me feel a bit sad.

"Oh no!" gasped Frankie. "It's 5.02pm. We're late!" I put my hand to my forehead in mock despair.

"Oh no! How could we be so irresponsible?" I cried. "Rosie will never forgive us!"

"Now girls," warned mum quite sternly. "Don't go upsetting Rosie. Oh look, here come Lyndz and Fliss."

Lyndz's dad drew up in his large van and Lyndz and Fliss leapt out.

"We're late!" they both shouted and we all laughed. We were all wearing our special badges and we felt pretty cool.

We started walking up the path and a huge gust of wind hit us. It lifted Fliss so far off the ground that she looked as though she was flying!

"I always knew you were a witch Fliss!" I laughed.

"You're too skinny," said Lyndz digging her in the ribs. "You need building up."

Fliss looked a bit flustered, then

kept saying, "Did you see me fly? I actually got right off the ground. Did you see?"

Frankie and I looked at each other and rolled our eyes. We would *never* hear the end of it now!

When we got to Rosie's front door, there was a soggy piece of paper stuck to it. It said 'TIMETABLE' in smudged ink. The first item – 'Outdoor Games' – had been crossed out.

"Oh dear!" muttered Frankie.

Rosie came to the door, even before we'd knocked.

"Sorry we're late," we all said together.

"Doesn't matter," mumbled Rosie. "You'd better come in."

It was almost as gloomy inside the house as it was outside.

"Hi Adam!" I called, seeing Rosie's brother in the hall. He just nodded. You remember Adam don't you? He's got cerebral palsy, and is in a wheelchair. He's got a wicked sense of humour and he's usually heaps of fun. Not on Saturday he wasn't. He just sulked in a corner and looked miserable.

"What's up with him?" I asked Rosie as we went up to her bedroom.

"Dad promised to take him fishing, but he had to cancel. He had a big job to finish or something." Rosie sounded miserable too.

We all looked anxiously at each other behind Rosie's back. Somehow this wasn't turning out to be the fun birthday party we'd expected.

"Where shall we put our presents?" asked Fliss.

"There's a big sack in the room next to the bathroom. I've put mine in it already. If the rest of you put yours in, mum said I could lock the door and then get the presents out again at bedtime," explained Rosie.

"Cool!"

We'd all arranged to wrap our presents in brown paper so that they would all look similar. We sneaked out of Rosie's bedroom separately and put the presents in the sack. When it was my turn I had a feel at the ones that were already in there. They all felt very interesting, but I couldn't tell what anything was. I couldn't find mine either!

When we had all put our presents in the sack, Rosie locked the door and put the key under her pillow.

"Right then Batman. What have you got planned instead of outdoor games?" I asked Rosie.

"Well, I haven't really," she muttered.

"What! Nothing planned?" I shrieked. "That's outrageous! We expect better of you Miss Cartwright! Don't we girls!" The others looked very serious and nodded.

Rosie began to smile.

"Well I thought maybe we could play 'Hide and Seek'," she said quietly. "If that's alright with you."

"Cool!"

"Wicked!"

"Brill!"

Rosie looked happy again. Then Tiffany, her sister, burst into the room.

"I hope you lot aren't going to be noisy all afternoon!" she snapped.

Noisy? That wasn't noisy! She hadn't heard anything yet! Her boyfriend, Spud, appeared in the doorway behind her.

"Aw Tiff, give them a break," he said. "Let them have a laugh."

Still scowling, she walked downstairs after him.

"What's her problem?" asked Frankie.

"Mum's had to go somewhere for one of her assignments at college. And she's left Tiff and Spud in charge until she gets back. Tiff is not very pleased!" explained Rosie. She looked as though she was going to get miserable again, so I said,

"I'll be 'it'. 1,2,3,..."

The others screamed and I could hear them scampering away to hide.

"...99,100. Coming! Ready or not!"

Rosie's house is a pretty cool house to hide in – but not such a great place to do the seeking in! There seem to be so many secret places that you just couldn't possibly know about. Usually Adam is a great help to whoever is seeking. He kind of gestures with his head, and creeps up behind you silently in his wheelchair and moves to where someone is hiding.

"Any clues Adam?" I called to him when I passed him in the hallway. But he just sat there looking sad. Surely Rosie's father's job couldn't have been that important. If Adam were my son, I'd always take him fishing when I promised him that I would.

"Hic!"

Lyndz is always easy to find. The excitement gets to her, then she starts hiccuping.

"Easy-peasy!" I told her. Then she giggled even more and went bright red.

"Honestly Lyndz. What are you

like!" I laughed. "Come on. Help me find the others."

We eventually found Frankie in a cloakroom downstairs. She was under a pile of coats and it was only her big feet that gave her away! I would recognise those trainers anywhere! Rosie was harder to find, but that's not surprising when it's her house and she knows all its secret places. There's a staircase, which leads to more rooms in the roof, and sort of tucked underneath it is a tiny hiding space. We only found it by accident because Lyndz tripped over and fell into it.

"Ouch!" cried a voice. We'd found Rosie!

After another half an hour of looking we still hadn't found Fliss. And we were bored. We shouted that we were giving up the search.

"Do you suppose she's heard us?" asked Rosie.

"'Course she has!" I said. "She just wants to make us sweat. Let's go and play something else. She'll come to us when she's fed up!"

"What time is it anyway?" asked Lyndz.

"Time you learnt to tell the time yourself!" Frankie and I shouted together.

"It's just after six," said Rosie. "That means it's almost time for doing makeovers."

"Can't we play something else first?" I pleaded. Hopefully, we'd get so involved in another game, the others would forget about the stupid makeovers.

"Let's play 'Tell Me'," said Rosie. "I've set it up in the lounge, just in case."

"Crikey Rosie. You've thought of everything haven't you?" said Frankie. You could see she was impressed. After that, Rosie's face was just one huge grin. If Frankie was impressed by her organisation, she was on to a winner!

We were in full flow with 'Tell Me',

yelling and shouting at each other, when the door opened. In came Fliss. Boy, did she look angry!

"Where've *you* been then?" I asked her as I spun the wheel.

"Hiding. I thought we were playing 'Hide and Seek'. I must have been wrong." Her mouth was set in a thin, tight line and she spat the words out.

"Keep your hair on!" I said. "Didn't you hear us calling to tell you that we gave up. Where were you hiding anyway?"

"In a cupboard in the bathroom. And it was very hot and very spooky in there by myself!"

"Come and sit down, Fliss. You can play with me if you want," said Rosie.

"I thought *you* might have waited for me," Fliss turned on Rosie. Rosie's smile disappeared again. She looked sadder than ever. The rest of us gave Fliss some of our 'black looks'. It had taken us ages to cheer Rosie up, trust Fliss to spoil it.

"What?" asked Fliss. "Why are you all looking at me like that?"

"Because…"

But we couldn't finish because an enormous CRASH shook the room and we all started to scream.

CHAPTER SEVEN

While we were screaming, two things seemed to happen together: firstly, we noticed that the large window in the lounge had shattered, and secondly, Rosie's mother appeared.

"Mum! What have you done?" Rosie wailed. She was staring at her mother as though she had just made her entrance by leaping through the window.

"Darling are you alright?" asked Mrs Cartwright. "Are you all alright? You haven't been cut by flying glass have you? Are you sure?" She was looking at us all anxiously.

"Why did you do that?" asked Rosie. She was still in a state of shock.

"Do what?" asked Rosie's mum. "I was just coming in the front door when there was an enormous gust of wind. I heard it shattering the window and I came in here. I didn't realise that you were here. Are you sure that you're alright?"

She looked at us carefully, checking for cuts. I was all prepared with my First Aid if anyone needed any assistance. Unfortunately they didn't.

"Did the wind make you fly?" asked Fliss. "It made me fly, didn't it Frankie?" Frankie sighed and nodded.

"No, I'm afraid I didn't fly Fliss," said Rosie's mum. "But that certainly sounds like fun." Fliss smiled and nodded. Rosie began to cry.

"Oh-oh," I muttered under my breath.

"What's the matter darling?" asked her mum, putting an arm around

Rosie's shaking shoulders.

"It's not fair!" cried Rosie. "Why does everything always go wrong for me? I wanted this sleepover to be perfect. I bet it wouldn't even have rained if it had been at someone else's house. But whenever *I* do anything, it always goes wrong."

"Don't be silly darling," said her mum. "It would have been raining today, wherever the sleepover had been."

"Yes and we wouldn't have had such a great time playing 'Hide and Seek' at anyone else's house," said Lyndz. "Your house is best for that."

Fliss tutted. She still hadn't forgiven us for leaving her, and something told me it would be a long time before she did.

"Yes, but what about the window?" said Rosie. "I bet that wouldn't have happened at one of your houses."

"That could have happened anywhere with this wind," Mrs

79

Cartwright reassured her. "It's just that our house is quite old, and some of the windows need replacing."

Rosie lost it completely when she said that.

"It's not fair. S'not fair," she sobbed. It was awful. I felt bad for Rosie and everything. But I couldn't see what the big deal was. I'd love it if a window smashed in our lounge. Nothing like that ever happens at my house.

Tiff and Spud appeared with brushes and newspaper and bin liners.

"Thanks you two," said Mrs Cartwright. "You can sweep the glass into a pile, but leave it for me to pick up."

Tiff sighed and stomped off with the brush.

"I'm just going to phone your father to see if he'll come round and board up the window..." continued Rosie's mum. Rosie let out another howl. "...You girls go upstairs to Rosie's room," said Mrs Cartwright, shooing us through the door, "and I'll call you when your food's ready."

We all trooped off upstairs. Frankie and Lyndz had their arms around Rosie. Fliss was pretending to fly up the stairs. And I was thinking what a crummy party this was turning out to be. It wasn't Rosie's fault, it was just that everyone seemed so *wet* sometimes. What we needed was a good old Gladiator fight or something. But when I suggested it Frankie went ballistic.

"Kenny, for goodness sake! Can't you see how upset Rosie is? I don't think bashing each other about is exactly what she needs right now!" she said.

So much for that idea. I knew that I could do with bashing someone about to make me feel better.

It was pretty gloomy in Rosie's room. We had to turn on the light even though it wasn't very late. The dark sky and rain outside made it feel like

November again.

I hate it when everyone is really quiet. I felt that I should say something to break the silence.

"The way that window smashed! It was way cool!" I said. The others shot me a look.

"Kenny!" warned Frankie. "Shut up can't you?"

"Sorry for breathing!" I snapped back. What was wrong with everybody?

"It's going to look like a squat isn't it?" mumbled Rosie through her tears.

"What do you mean?" asked Lyndz.

"With the window boarded up. Everybody's going to think that I live in some run-down shack," Rosie wailed.

"Don't be silly!" I said. "It'll only be for one night, then someone can replace the window tomorrow, or Monday at the latest. No one's even going to notice it." Rosie stopped crying.

"Actually Rosie, you look pretty awful," I laughed. "We'll have to do something about those red eyes. It's just not a good look for you, darling!" The others laughed too.

"Come on then Fliss. Do your stuff with that make-up!" I said.

"Are you having make-up on as well?" asked Rosie.

I could feel the others all staring at me. Now you know me and make-up. Yeuch! is all I can say. But this was an exception, and I only did it for Rosie because she was so upset. I'll admit it: for the first – and last – time, I let Fliss make me up. The others were more bothered about that than having their own make-up done. And usually they all argue about who should have theirs done first and which eye shadow they should wear. On the birthday Saturday, they stood about watching me with their chins scraping the floor. I mean p-lease! Anyone would think I was some rare animal in a zoo or something.

"So, how do I look?" I asked pouting

and posing like a model.

"Wicked!"

"Coo-el!"

"You really ought to wear it more often. It really suits you," said Fliss standing back to admire her handiwork.

"Ta very much!" I shrieked, pretending to be upset. "Are you saying that I'm ugly the rest of the time?"

"Well yes actually, we are!" Frankie laughed.

I grabbed her by the arms and wrestled her to the floor. That was more like it! Everyone seemed to be having fun, piling on top of us and shrieking. It was almost worth the embarrassment of wearing blue eyeshadow and pink lipstick to have everyone back to normal again. But I knew that it was too good to last. The light suddenly flickered, then it went out completely.

We were all in a pile on the floor and

I was at the bottom. So I thought I was going to get squashed when Fliss started screaming and didn't move. What is it about lights going out that makes people scream? I mean, what did she really think was going to happen? Did she honestly think that there was some monster lurking about who had turned out the lights so it could come in and eat us all up? I don't think so.

"Fliss! Shut up and get up!" I gasped.

By that time Rosie had started screaming too. Thank goodness Frankie is a bit more together. She forced her way out of the pile of bodies and stumbled to the window. We could see that it was completely dark outside – no street lights, nothing.

"It's OK," she said. "Nobody's got any lights on. There must have been a power cut!"

We all crowded round the window to have a look out. It's funny isn't it?

You think you know somewhere really well, but when you look at it differently, like when there are no lights on, it's like you're seeing it for the first time. Rosie's front garden looked massive. And because it had been raining so hard, it looked as though there was a stream running down the middle of it.

"This is wicked!" I said.

"It's a bit spooky!" said Fliss, shivering.

The door creaked open. We all jumped about a mile. All we could see at first was a light shining towards us.

"Are you alright girls?" It was Mrs Cartwright. "It's only a power cut. Have you brought your torches? I could only find this one."

We always take our torches to sleepovers. We scrambled about in our sleeping bags and found them.

"Do you want to come downstairs and stay with us until your food's ready?" asked Rosie's mum.

"No thanks Mum. We'll be fine up here," said Rosie.

"OK I'll call you. It won't be long," said her mum and closed the door behind her.

"Rosie, this is so cool!" Lyndz squeaked, hugging Rosie.

You could tell that Rosie wished she'd planned the whole thing herself. At last the tenth birthday sleepover was turning into a party worth remembering!

CHAPTER EIGHT

Rosie has this big double bed in her bedroom. But then you probably remember that, right? Well, it was really cool, because we could all sit on it and spook each other out. We held the torches under our chins and pulled gruesome faces. Fliss kept screaming and hiding her face in Rosie's shoulder. What is she like?

Then we started to tell ghost stories and that *really* scared Fliss. She kept screaming "Shut up! Please shut up!" But of course the more she did that, the more we thought of even spookier stories. Frankie's brill at all that stuff, but she knows she is and acts really cool about it.

"There was once a haunted house, very much like Rosie's house actually," she started. Nobody moved. "It had lots of rooms, it had cellars and attics, very much like here. And under the attic stairs there was a secret passage that no one knew about. Except the ghost!"

We all squealed a bit and huddled closer together.

"It was the ghost of a man who used to live in the house. It was the only place he'd ever been happy. So he slid through the walls and watched over the family who lived there now. They never saw the ghost, they just felt an icy chill whenever he came into the room."

We huddled closer together still, so that we could almost feel each other breathing.

"One day the girl of the house, who

was very much like Rosie, was in her bedroom with some of her friends when..."

Rosie's bedroom door squeaked open and a rush of cold air filled the room. We all screamed with fright. We clung to each other and kept our heads down. If that was the ghost, we didn't want to see him.

"Well, I know I'm irresistible girls, but I didn't know I was *that* irresistible!" It was only Spud. "Your mum asked me to tell you that 'grub's up'!"

I could feel my heart booming inside my chest. I didn't think it would ever get back to normal.

"That was chilling, Frankie!" I told her.

"How did you arrange with Spud to come in at just the right moment?" asked Fliss. You could tell she was still shaken, but she was desperate not to let the rest of us see.

"Well, you know Fliss, I didn't,"

Frankie said very seriously. "I reckon the ghost must have told him when to come in!"

"Aaah! Frankie don't say that!" Fliss seemed to have gone very pale, although it was hard to tell by torchlight.

We all trooped downstairs, stumbling a bit as we went. Tiffany was at the bottom of the stairs, shining a torch to show us the way into the dining room.

"Hey Tiff, you could get a job in the cinema," laughed Rosie.

"Shut your face!" said her sister, but even she looked happier than she had done earlier.

Eating is one of my favourite things, after Leicester City of course, and I was getting very hungry. It seemed like the others were too, because we all barged into each other and bundled into the dining room. We couldn't believe what we saw there. It was mega-wicked. Everywhere was glowing with candlelight. There were loads of candles in jam jars down the middle of the table and on the fireplace. There were even a couple of lanterns hanging in the window.

"Oh wow!" said Rosie. "This is brilliant, Mum!"

The rest of us gasped and just stood there gawping. It was like we couldn't even move.

"I know that I don't need to tell you this, because I know that you're all sensible girls," said Mrs Cartwright. "But candles are dangerous, so I don't want you touching them. OK? Right, lecture over. Who's for pizza!"

"Me!" we all shouted and made a dive for the table.

In the other room we could hear voices. One was Spud's.

"Is Dad here?" Rosie called to her mum.

"Yes, he's just doing the window. Spud and Adam are helping him," she called back.

"I'd forgotten about that," said Rosie glumly.

"Don't worry," I told her. "It's so dark we won't even be able to see it."

"I suppose not," she said, but she'd gone all sad again.

"Oh come on Rosie, cheer up!" said Frankie. "This is one of the best parties I've ever been to. And it hasn't really started yet! What's next on your timetable?"

Rosie pulled out a scruffy bit of paper from her pocket. She held it up to one of the lanterns on the table.

"Oh no!" she yelled, slamming her fist down. "I didn't think anything else could go wrong!"

"What's up?" I asked. "Don't tell me we've run over time with the meal! We haven't even had the cake yet!"

"Nope. It's worse than that," sighed Rosie shoving the paper back in her pocket. "I'd got everything ready for a disco..."

"We can dance by candlelight. It'll

be cool!" shouted Lyndz.

"There's just one little problem," mumbled Rosie.

"What?" we all asked.

"No power. How can we play my cassettes if we've no electricity?"

She was right. That certainly was a problem.

"How come your mum's cooked the pizza and garlic bread if there's still a power cut?" asked Fliss.

"We've got a gas cooker Fliss," said Mrs Cartwright who had just come in to collect our plates.

"Mum..." Rosie called, but she'd gone out of the room again.

"We could play Twister by candlelight," suggested Frankie. "It'll be a laugh."

"I suppose we'll have to," said Rosie. "Unless anybody can think of something else we can do instead."

"I know!" I shouted. "Let's have the birthday cake! Seeing as I helped to make it!"

"You?" shouted the others.

"I don't think holding a sieve actually counts as 'helping' does it?" asked Frankie. I was suddenly bombarded by handfuls of crisps and popcorn. Charming! So that's all the thanks I get for losing my cred in the kitchen!

"Oi! Watch it you lot!" shouted Tiffany.

We looked up. She had just come into the room and was carrying our cake. Ten candles were flickering on top of it. It was class! I know we'd all seen birthday cakes before, but this was really special. It might have been because we'd made the cake ourselves. Or it might have been because the room looked pretty cool anyway with all the other candles. Whatever it was, for a few moments none of us could speak. Then we all sort of squealed together. I know that it sounds a bit nerdy now. I guess you just had to be there.

"We've all got to blow the candles out together and make a wish," said Fliss.

So we sang *'Happy birthday to us, Happy Birthday to us, Happy Birthday dear Sleepover Club, Happy Birthday to us!'*, then we all took an enormous breath and whoosh! All the candles were blown out. I can't tell you what I wished for, obviously, or else it won't come true. But you can have a guess.

As far as the actual cake was concerned, well, I'd be lying to you if I said it was the best cake I'd ever tasted. But it wasn't too bad. None of us went down with food poisoning anyway.

When we'd all finished, Rosie said "Right then, we might as well go into the lounge and play Twister."

Tiff, who was clearing up the table, shouted "No! Not yet!" just like that. It was really weird.

"Why not?" asked Rosie, sounding a bit miffed.

"Because..." spluttered her sister.

"Because Tiffany's been helping me all evening and she thought that you could all help to clear the table," explained Rosie's mum.

We didn't mind doing that, and she was right, Tiff had been helping out with the food and everything. I'm sure that she would rather have been out with Spud somewhere. She hadn't even grumbled about it either.

While we were taking the plates and stuff into the kitchen, Rosie's mum went into the lounge. We could hear whispering and giggling.

"I bet Mum wants to join in with Twister," said Rosie in a quiet voice. "She keeps telling me that it's one of her favourite games."

"You should let her. It'll be fun," I said. I couldn't see either of my parents wanting to join in with something like that. But Rosie's mum is pretty cool.

"It's *embarrassing*!" Rosie hissed, just as her mum came back into the kitchen.

"What's embarrassing?" she asked.

"Me always wearing my football shirt," I said quickly.

"It's not embarrassing," laughed Rosie's mum. "If that's what you want to wear, then you go right ahead and wear it Kenny. Stand up for what you believe in, that's what I say." Rosie rolled her eyes.

"Anyway, thank you girls," Rosie's mum continued, taking a pile of plates from Fliss. "You go into the lounge and do whatever you're going to do. I might join in with Twister myself!"

"What did I tell you?" Rosie muttered under her breath.

We grabbed our torches and stumbled across the hall into the lounge. When Rosie opened the door, there was a loud blast of music and a flash of coloured lights. It looked like a proper disco! Mega-cool or what!

CHAPTER NINE

Rosie's dad, Adam and Spud were at the far end of the lounge. They all had great goofy grins on their faces.

"I thought there was a power cut!" shouted Rosie above the Spice Girls, who were blaring out from the cassette player.

"There was, but the electricity came on again just before you had your meal," explained Rosie's dad. "Your mum thought it would be nice if we surprised you with all this."

The Christmas lights, which were strung up around the walls, were flashing in time to the music.

"Spud helped me with those," said Mr Cartwright, "and Adam helped with the music, didn't you son?" Adam grinned and nodded.

"It's brill!" Rosie gave her dad and Adam a big kiss, and punched Spud on the arm in a friendly way.

Rosie's mum and Tiff had appeared in the doorway.

"Thanks Mum!" Rosie called and blew her a kiss.

Her mum smiled and said, "But I thought we were going to play Twister!"

"Later Mum!" Rosie laughed and pulled a face at the rest of us.

Rosie's dad didn't look as though he was the kind of man who likes to dance. He looked a bit embarrassed watching us too. I'm a fling-myself-all-over-the-room kind of dancer, and when I'd trodden on his toes a few times he decided that it was time he made a move. As far away from us as possible!

"Bye girls! Have a good party!" he called. Rosie looked disappointed to see him leaving. I think she thought it was nice to have all her family round her for once. I guess she wants her parents to get back together, but I don't think they will. They seem kind of happy without each other.

"Thanks Mr Cartwright!" we shouted to Rosie's dad. "This is wicked!" Rosie just stood there looking sad.

"Come on Rosie! Get with the groove!" I shouted and got her dancing again.

At least Adam was smiling again. He was kind of whizzing backwards and forwards in his wheelchair as though he was dancing with us.

"Hey, what have you got there?" I asked him. He had a box resting on his knee. He moved closer so that I could see it. It was a CD-Rom all about football. It was way cool!

"You lucky thing! Did your dad bring it for you?" I asked. Adam nodded.

"Monster!"

Adam is really hot on the computer. He has a good one because it's a kind of therapy for him. Rosie and Tiff use it too of course, but it's in Adam's room and he seems to use it the most. He had to show Rosie's mum how to use it when she started college, which we all thought was funny. It's usually parents who show their kids how to do stuff isn't it? But with computers it always seems to be the other way round!

"Did Dad bring you that because he didn't take you fishing?" asked Rosie dancing up to us. Adam nodded.

"That's not fair is it?" she said grumpily.

"He probably realised how disappointed Adam was," I said.

"Yeah well. It's not the same is it?" Rosie said crossly.

"Chill out!" I laughed. "Adam's happy *and* your dad set all this up," I said pointing to the lights. "You can't have a downer on him today!" Rosie looked a bit guilty. "Suppose not," she said and danced over to the others.

"Aren't we playing Twister then?" called out Mrs Cartwright.

"No Mum!" laughed Rosie.

"Well anyway, 'dancing's what I want, what I really really want'," sang Rosie's mum in time to the music. "I think I love dancing more than I love Twister, anyway."

Rosie groaned but you could tell that she was secretly pleased that her mum was so trendy. And her mum was brill. You'd think *she* was the schoolgirl, the way she screamed with laughter all the time. But she wasn't embarrassing or anything. I still think that Rosie sometimes wishes her mum would act her age more.

After she'd been dancing for half an hour or so, Mrs Cartwright flopped onto the settee. "Phew! I'm exhausted. I think I need a lie-down!" she gasped, "and speaking of lying down..." She looked at her watch, "it's almost nine now. Another half an hour then it's time you lot started making tracks upstairs."

"Aw Mum! You said ten!" pleaded Rosie, looking at her mum with her eyes all wide.

"Don't push it my girl!" laughed her mum. "If you're good – we'll see!"

"Cool!" we all yelled and did high fives.

Rosie's mum went out and we expected Tiff and Spud to follow, but they didn't, they stayed behind.

"It's alright," Rosie told them. "We're not going to wreck the place. We don't need to be chaperoned any more!"

"We thought we might stay, actually. This *is* my cassette you're playing," mumbled Tiff.

We were listening to Oasis, which was class. Tiff and Spud started dancing – if you could call it that. Spud sort of jerked around the floor and Tiff shuffled along behind him. Very strange! Rosie shrugged her shoulders as if to say 'I'm sorry about them, but what can I do?' But the rest of us didn't mind. The more the merrier, and Tiff and Spud were alright really. Adam stayed for a short while, but then Rosie's mum came in to get him ready for bed. He sort of waved 'Goodbye' to us all. I'm glad that he'd joined in with our party.

Time seems to flash past when you're having fun doesn't it? We couldn't believe it when Rosie's mum came in and told us that it was nearly ten. Lyndz was starting to look a bit dopey and Fliss had been slumped on the settee for the last fifteen minutes or so. But the rest of us were full of beans and ready to dance the night away.

"Not in this house you don't!" laughed Rosie's mum. "Right, quick sticks, upstairs and ready for bed. And I don't want to hear a peep out of you."

She looked at us and laughed. "Some hope!"

We'd had a great day. Better than we'd expected when we first arrived. And everyone seemed really happy, especially Rosie.

"Great party, Rosie!" said Frankie, when we got up to the bedroom.

"Yeah, monster!" I agreed.

Fliss and Lyndz had already crashed out on the bed, but they mumbled their appreciation too.

Speaking of crashing out on the bed, we hadn't decided who was going to sleep where. When we have a sleepover at Rosie's, three of us manage to fit on her double bed and the other two have to sleep on the floor. It's only fair that Rosie has the bed seeing as it's her house, and the rest of us usually toss for it. Only this time it looked as though Fliss and Lyndz were already settled down for the night. They still had to get undressed and do all the bathroom stuff. But even I wasn't mean enough to make them sleep on the floor.

"It looks like you and me kid!" I said to Frankie in my fake American accent. She just groaned. Cheeky thing!

I can't work Fliss out sometimes. We virtually had to carry her into the bathroom because she was so tired, but when we got back into our sleeping bags and someone mentioned the magic words, "Is it time for our presents now?" Whoosh! She was wide-awake and raring to go.

"Presents! I'd almost forgotten about our presents! Go and get them Rosie!" she yelled.

"OK. Keep your hair on!" said Rosie and felt under her pillow for the room's key.

"Right, who's the joker?" she demanded. "Whoever's got the key, can you give it back now? Please."

We all looked at each other. Or rather everyone looked at me. I do sometimes hide things for a joke, I'll admit. But not this time. Besides, I'd never been alone in the bedroom, so I couldn't have taken the key. Come to think of it, we'd all been together since we got there. Apart from Fliss. She'd been by herself for half an hour or more when we left her during Hide and Seek.

"OK Fliss, we know you've got it. Hand it over!" I said, half-joking. We were all totally gob-smacked when Fliss went very red and started to cry.

CHAPTER TEN

"I haven't got the key," Fliss sobbed. "I *did* look for it when you lot left me during Hide and Seek, but I couldn't find it. I'm sorry."

"Well what would you have done if you had found it?" I demanded.

"I don't know. Just felt the presents I suppose," Fliss mumbled through her sniffs.

"That's a bit sneaky Fliss," said Frankie. "We were all supposed to get our presents together."

"And now none of us can get them because we've lost the key," said Rosie crossly.

"Look I've said I'm sorry, haven't I?" cried Fliss. "I wouldn't have taken them or anything."

"I know you wouldn't," said Rosie more gently. "Maybe the key fell off the bed when you were feeling for it." We all got down on our hands and knees and shone our torches under the bed. The key wasn't there, but there were several large gaps between the floorboards.

"Maybe it's fallen down there," said Frankie.

We pushed Rosie's bed to one side and Rosie shone her torch down the gaps. "I can see it!" she said. "Who's going to put their hand down to pull it out?"

We all looked at Fliss. She'd got us into this mess, and she probably had the smallest hands to get us out!

"It feels all dusty and horrible!" she grumbled as she fished about under the floorboards.

"Yeah, watch out for the mice!" I laughed.

Fliss, who had just grabbed hold of the key, screamed, pulled her arm out of the floorboards and let go of the key. CLINK! We heard it landing somewhere at the other side of the room.

"Oh well done Fliss!" I snarled.

"It was your fault for making me jump!" she snapped back.

"Oh for goodness sake stop it you two!" said Frankie. "I can see the key by the door." She went and picked it up. "There. Right, who's for presents?"

"ME!" we all shouted.

"I'll get them," said Rosie. She took the key from Frankie and crept out of the door.

When she was out of the room, Mrs Cartwright came in.

"Not in bed yet girls?" she asked. "I thought you might need these." She tipped a carrier bag on to the bed. Our midnight feast!

"Thanks Mrs Cartwright!" we said.

"That's OK. Just don't make yourselves sick. And don't stay awake too long. Where's Rosie-Posie?"

"Here!" Rosie had just come back into the bedroom, carrying the plastic sack full of presents.

"Ooh, your presents!" said her mum, smiling. "I might stay to watch you opening those!"

One look at Rosie's face made her change her mind!

"On second thoughts, I could do with going to bed. Have fun! And try not to make too much noise!" Mrs Cartwright went out, closing the door behind her.

"Why don't we have our midnight feast while we open our presents?" asked Frankie. "It'll be cool!"

We all went to sit on Rosie's bed and spread the sweets out in the middle. There were Black Jacks, fizzy fish, rhubarb and crumble sweets, a Mars bar, some Doritos and a big bag of popcorn. Scrummy!

As we started to munch into

everything, Rosie delved into her sack and pulled out the first present.

"Frankie!" she announced, and tossed a parcel towards her. It looked quite big and lumpy. It was impossible to guess what it might be.

"Go on! Open it!" shouted Fliss.

"No, I'm going to wait until we've all got our presents, then we can open them together," said Frankie. Typical! I'd have ripped into mine straight away. Now we'd *all* have to wait until everyone had got one.

"Come on then Rosie. Hurry up!" I was getting as bad as Fliss!

Rosie handed a big, flat parcel to Lyndz. It looked quite heavy, but you couldn't tell what it was. She kept a scrunched up parcel for herself which sort of rattled when she touched it. When she gave Fliss hers, you could tell she was just dying to open it. She kept squeezing it and putting it close to her ear and shaking it. I had to turn away because I was dying to laugh and

I didn't want her to know that it was from me. My present was the last out of the sack. It was soft and squashy, but it kind of rattled too, in a muffled sort of way.

"On your marks! Get set!" shouted Rosie, her parcel in her hand. "GO!"

We all ripped into the brown paper. My present had about a whole roll of sellotape on it, so it wasn't easy to get at.

"Look at this! My own baby sister!" shrieked Frankie. She was holding a gross-looking baby doll. It was all squashy and looked as though it was about to puke any minute. But Frankie loved it.

"Look it's got a bottle too. Can I fill it with water?" she yelled and rushed out to the bathroom.

"Whoever bought her that got it right!" I laughed. "But you do realise, we'll now have a sixth member of the Sleepover Club. She'll take it everywhere with her!"

"I'd never have thought of that for Frankie," said Fliss. "She always seems too grown up for dolls!"

Frankie rushed back into the room,

"Look at this!" she yelled. "It's so cool!"

She gave the baby its bottle and it started to wee.

"Oh gross!" I said. Only Frankie could be thrilled with that.

"Oh wow!" gasped Fliss. "Look at these bangles. Wicked! I saw these in Miss Selfridge. They're brill! You got them for me didn't you, Rosie? Thanks, they're great!"

Monster! She actually thought that someone had bought them! Fortunately when she said that I had just opened my present, which was a wicked pair of Leicester City socks. I shoved them in my mouth to stop myself laughing at Fliss, and I nearly choked on the Fox keyring, which was wrapped up inside them.

"Oh man! This is so cool!" I

shrieked, bouncing up and down on Rosie's bed. I looked round at the others, but it was impossible to tell who had bought them for me.

"I bet this was from you Fliss, wasn't it?" asked Rosie. She was looking at some frosted eyeshadow, and matching lipstick and nail varnish. Fliss blushed and nodded.

"Thank you!" said Rosie hugging her. "I always have to borrow Tiff's make-up and now I've got some of my very own!"

Lyndz was still trying to unfasten her present. Frankie leaned across to help her. When they finally ripped off the paper, we could see that it was a handmade wooden door plaque, which read: 'LYNDZ'S ROOM'. Underneath someone had painted: 'Keep Out Stuart, Tom, Ben and Spike'.

"This is great!" yelled Lyndz. "Now they've no excuse to barge into my room!"

We looked at each other's presents

and tried to guess who had bought them. But apart from Fliss admitting that she'd bought Rosie's make-up, no one was letting on.

Frankie was still shaking with laughter at her doll, when Mrs Cartwright appeared. She was in her dressing gown and had taken her make-up off. She didn't look quite as young and trendy as she usually did. And she sounded very tired.

"Come on you lot! Some of us have assignments to finish tomorrow!" she sighed.

"Sorry!" we all said, and got into our sleeping bags.

"Night!" she called and turned the light out. We counted to twenty-five, then turned on our torches.

"Thanks for a great party Rosie," Frankie whispered.

"It has been good hasn't it?" Rosie whispered back. And it had. After a lousy start!

We sang our Club song, turned off

our torches and settled down to sleep. Frankie had her sleeping bag right next to mine on the floor.

"Did you get me my socks?" I whispered.

"I'm not saying anything," she laughed. I thought she might have done, but then I thought that I recognised her writing on Lyndz's plaque.

"Who do you think bought you the doll?" I asked, but she was already asleep. I could see her 'baby' tucked up beside her. Sweet! A bit sad, but sweet all the same!

The next morning when we woke up – wouldn't you know it, – the sun was shining! We played the outdoor games we should have played at the party. Then, after breakfast, it was time for us to go. Fliss's mum came to collect Fliss and Lyndz. Fliss was wearing her bracelets. I was well-chuffed about that, but I didn't let on that I'd made them. What she doesn't know won't hurt her, as Frankie's gran says.

Frankie and I walked home together. We were already planning what we should do for our twentieth birthday sleepover! We agreed that Rosie's party had been pretty cool, and that the bad things like the rain and the power cut are what had made it special. It just goes to show that however much you plan something, it never turns out as you expect it to.

So now you know all about our tenth birthday sleepover party! Come on, I'll race you to Frankie's! She's going to be so mad when she finds out that I've already told you all about it. But too much talking would only have made her sore throat worse! I reckon she only got it because she shrieked so much over that stupid doll. I wonder if she's figured out who gave it to her yet. I *think* I might have worked out who gave everybody their presents but I'm not completely sure. What do you think?

Come on! Last one to Frankie's is a pile of slime!

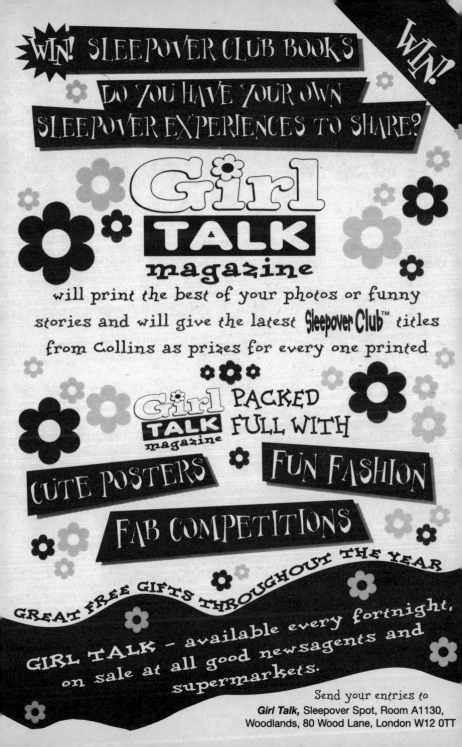

The Sleepover Club at Frankie's

Join the Sleepover Club: Frankie, Kenny, Felicity, Rosie and Lyndsey, five girls who just want to have fun – but who always end up in mischief.

Brown Owl's in a bad mood and the Sleepover Club are determined to cheer her up. Maybe she'd be happier if she had a new boyfriend. And where better than a sleepover at Frankie's to plan Operation Blind Date?

Pack up your sleepover kit and drop in on the fun!

0 00 675233 0
£2. 99

The Sleepover Club at Rosie's

Join the Sleepover Club: Frankie, Kenny, Felicity, Rosie and Lyndsey, five girls who just want to have fun – but who always end up in mischief.

The Pet Show should be really exciting for the girls except that Fliss doesn't have a pet! But, for the Sleepover Club who can outwit their dastardly enemies, the M&Ms, that shouldn't be a big problem – should it?

Pack up your sleepover kit and drop in on the fun!

0 00 675235 7
£2. 99

The Sleepover Club at Lyndsey's

Join the Sleepover Club: Frankie, Kenny, Felicity, Rosie and Lyndsey, five girls who just want to have fun – but who always end up in mischief.

The girls plan a great party for Lyndsey's birthday – fun, food, a spooky video and a sleepover. Definitely not for boys! But somehow Lyndsey's brothers make their presence felt and soon everyone's too scared to sleep.

Pack up your sleepover kit and drop in on the fun!

0 00 675234 9
£2. 99

The 24-Hour Sleepover Club

Join the Sleepover Club: Frankie, Kenny, Felicity, Rosie and Lyndsey, five girls who just want to have fun – but who always end up in mischief.

It's the Sleepover anniversary, the most important date in their diary. The girls plan a visit to the fair and a picnic; sounds like a pleasant but uneventful sleepover, until they cross paths with their arch-rivals the M&M's... beware, low flying jellies!

Pack up your sleepover kit and drop in on the fun!

0 00 675336-1
£2. 99

The Sleepover Girls go Spice

Join the Sleepover Club: Frankie, Kenny, Felicity, Rosie and Lyndsey, five girls who just want to have fun – but who always end up in mischief.

'That's great, you sound just like them, there's five of you too...' Find out who's Top of the Flops when the Sleepover Club decide to launch themselves into the world of pop... and just who is that making a noise lke a crow?

Pack up your sleepover kit and drop in on the fun!

0 00 675346-9
£2. 99

Order Form

To order direct from the publishers, just make a list of the titles you want and fill in the form below:

Name

....

Address

....

....

....

Send to: Dept 6, HarperCollins Publishers Ltd, Westerhill Road, Bishopbriggs, Glasgow G64 2QT.

Please enclose a cheque or postal order to the value of the cover price, plus:

UK & BFPO: Add £1.00 for the first book, and 25p per copy for each additional book ordered.

Overseas and Eire: Add £2.95 service charge. Books will be sent by surface mail but quotes for airmail despatch will be given on request.

A 24-hour telephone ordering service is available to holders of Visa, MasterCard, Amex or Switch cards on 0141-772 2281.

Collins

An *Imprint of* HarperCollins*Publishers*